Turtleberry Press

Baltimore, MD 21234

www.turtleberrypress.com

Just before her fortieth birthday, Shayla loses her job and has to figure out what she wants to do with her life. Wayne was a one night stand she met at a conference, who also happens to be on the team who took over the company she worked for. Shayla, with the help of friends, decides it's time to pursue her dream career. She also decides to give Wayne a chance.

He was sitting at the table with the only available seat when I got to the mixer. I took that as a sign that I shouldn't be as upset as I was about running five minutes late. The man was gorgeous. My eyes were drawn to his dark brown eyes and freshly shaped up goatee. He had the most kissable lips, nice and plump but not too big. He smiled at me as I walked over. He moved his bag out of the seat.

"Thanks."

"You haven't missed much. I think she is going to make us do one of those awful ice breaker games."

I groaned and smiled. "Oh joy."

Before he could speak again, the moderator announced the icebreaker that he predicted. As awkward as it was, I at least learned that his name was Wayne and he was an executive with the company he worked for. Our table was a mix of staff, like me, and managers. The conference was on diversity and it was nice to see a good mix of people in this first session. After the icebreaker, she went right into her presentation. There was no real chance to say anything else to Wayne until after she was done. Then two other people at the table seemed to be lobbying for his attention. I decided to take that cue and head out to find some dinner. I hadn't eaten since breakfast. My flight was at two and that didn't give me any time to grab lunch and make it through airport security. Especially since my employer insisted that I come to work that morning.

"Shayla."

I stopped walking down the hall when I heard him call my name. His voice was so smooth I couldn't help but smile. I toned the smile down before turning around to face him. "Hi."

"I wanted to see if you wanted to grab dinner with a few of us."

"Um…"

"Did you already have plans?"

"No."

"So don't eat alone." He smiled at me. "Join us."

I wasn't sure who he was referring to but I couldn't help but want to spend more time looking at his face so I followed him down the hall. We met up with a group of about five others and headed across the street to a restaurant. Dinner was good and the conversation was all over the place and thankfully not on work. Everyone seemed content talking about conferences they had been to in the past. I was content hanging on the edge of the conversation while trying not to stare at Wayne. His voice was delicious. It gave me chills every time he spoke. It was hard to curb my hormones and focus on the conversation.

After dinner, Wayne walked next to me as the group headed back to the hotel. He was close enough for me to smell a hint of his cologne. He smelled refreshing and made me want to get even closer to him. I had to silently scold myself for wanting to bury my face in his neck. It had been far too long since I had my face in a good-smelling man's neck. I was both sad and thankful when we parted in the hotel elevator. He was on a different floor.

I decided to shower once I got in the room. My hope was to get my mind off Wayne but it didn't work out that way. As soon as I got in, my mind went right to him. I found myself trying to imagine what he looked like out of the suit he was in when I saw him. I imagined him to be exactly my type with a body that showed he knew where the gym was, and likely had a membership though he doesn't live there. The last guy I dated who was into the gym seemed to always make sure that he was in the gym when I was free to hang out and it had been a turn-off ever since.

There was nothing about the thought of Wayne turning me off. The shower did nothing to quell my imagination. That led to me being restless in the hotel room. I decided to get dressed and head down to the bar. I hoped that one or two glasses of wine would clear my head and allow me to sleep.

The bar wasn't crowded and I was able to get a table to myself. I tried not to sit at the bar when alone. It made it easier for people to approach you under the guise of standing next to you to order their drink. I knew it also wouldn't help that I had on a v-neck shirt that would cause most guys to stare at my boobs while coming up with whatever excuse to talk to me. I wanted to meet someone, just not like that.

Thoughts of meeting someone brought Wayne back to my mind and I shook my head. After a sip of wine, I decided to do the one thing that I knew would take my mind off of him. I checked my work email from my phone. The first email I saw was from my supervisor scheduling a meeting to debrief me on what happened at the conference. A conference that I was attending because he thought it wasn't worth his time. I rolled my eyes and moved on to the rest of the emails.

"Excuse me but it pains me to see you sitting all alone."

I glanced up at the guy. "It shouldn't."

"You're too beautiful to be sitting alone. Let me join you."

I held my hand up as he went to sit in the seat. "No. I don't want you to join me."

"But you shouldn't be alone."

I groaned and started to speak but stopped when I saw Wayne walk around the guy and sit in the seat the guy pulled out. Wayne handed me another glass of wine and smiled. I smiled back. "Thank you."

Wayne glanced at the guy for a moment. "Good to see you again Shawn."

The guy mumbled something and then walked away.

"You know him."

"I have had to check him a few times at a few conferences. He still hasn't learned how to approach a woman."

I laughed and put my phone down. "I didn't think I looked like I wanted to be approached."

"You didn't." Wayne sipped his drink. "I like to think I have saved him from extreme embarrassment."

"You did."

"My good deed for the day."

"Along with refilling my glass."

Wayne smiled and raised his glass. "I saw you when you got here but hated to interrupt."

"You did?"

"Yeah. I was at the bar with a few colleagues."

"I got bored and thought the wine might help me sleep."

"I started to actually do work and decided I needed to take a walk."

His voice warmed my insides. I sipped my wine to cool off but it felt more like fuel to the fire. My mind started to ponder if I could spend the night with him. I didn't know much about Wayne. I knew enough to know that he seemed perfect for what would hopefully be a wonderful evening. My mind was set on making it happen.

"I checked my email but that is as far as I'm going."

"Let's not talk about email. My inbox is a disaster area."

I laughed. "Okay. No talking about work."

"So, tell me about what you like to do for fun."

"I do a lot of things."

"Like?"

"Happy hours, sporting events, concerts, day parties, book club…"

"Paint nights?"

I laughed. "I love a good sip and paint."

Wayne chuckled. "Nothing wrong with that."

"My friends and I get together at least once or twice a week to do something fun."

"Same."

"What do y'all do?" I smiled. "Sip and paint?"

"No." He smiled. "We have a weekly basketball game we play. We go to sporting events and happy hours. I have been known to attend a party or two."

"As long as you don't sit in the house and spend all your free time playing video games."

Wayne laughed. "No. I play every so often but I like to get out and do things. I like to get away as much as work will allow."

"I want to take more trips."

"Where?"

"Everywhere." I smiled. "I wanted to get away for my birthday but I am settling on going out with friends."

"Your birthday is soon?"

"In a month."

"Nice."

I sipped my wine. "I wanted to do something bigger for this particular birthday."

"You got me curious even though I know it isn't polite to ask a woman's age."

"I'm turning forty."

"I would not have guessed."

"Good." I laughed.

"You look damn good for forty."

"I have a month to go."

"Something tells me you will only get better with time."

I blushed slightly. "From your lips to God's ears."

"Amen."

"And how old are you?"

"Forty-two."

"You also look good for your age."

"I try." He glanced at my empty glass. "Would you like another?"

"No thank you. Two is my conference limit."

"Ah. Okay."

"I should probably head back up to my room."

"May I escort you to the elevator?"

I smiled at him. "You don't want to make sure I get to my room safely."

He leaned closer to me. “I’d much rather make sure you got to my room safely but that might be pushing it a bit.”

“Maybe.” I stood up and looked down at him. “Maybe not.”

“Are you suggesting I press my luck?” Wayne stood up.

“Yes.”

Wayne took my hand and led me to the elevators. When we got on, we stood on opposite sides and just looked at each other. Wayne looked just as good in a polo shirt and khakis as he had in a suit. He was incredibly sexy. The way he looked at me turned me on even more. Going back to a stranger’s room wasn’t something that I ever thought I would do but I was really glad that I decided to do it. It felt like a jolt of electricity went through my body when he took my hand as the elevator arrived on his floor. He led me down the hall to his room.

Once we were inside, Wayne pulled me into his arms and kissed me. His lips were just as I imagined them, extremely soft. We stripped each other's clothes off and plopped down on his bed.

"I like to get the first orgasm out of the way." Wayne said as his hand slipped between my legs and his fingers immediately began massaging my clit.

I moaned as his lips moved to my neck. The man was very good with his hands. His other hand was massaging my breast. It didn't take long before I climaxed. I had my arm over my eyes as I caught my breath.

"Now I can take my time."

Before I could even regain my focus, Wayne was planting kisses on my thighs before burying his face in my pussy. I squealed as his tongue slipped inside of me. He spread my legs wide while he slowly feasted on me. It was overwhelmingly good. I wondered where Wayne had been all my life. My second orgasm was much more powerful than the first. I wanted to scream but my voice got caught in my throat.

Wayne gave me time to recover. I propped myself up on my elbows once I felt like I had it together. He was sitting next to me, condom already on, just watching me.

"You good?" He asked.

I reached for him, put my hand on his cheek, and guided him to me. We kissed softly at first but it slowly got more passionate. His lips moved to my neck and his hand gently grabbed my hair. He pulled and kissed me as he eased his dick inside of me. As he moved inside me, I rocked my hips and met each and every stroke. Wayne kept one hand in my hair and the other had him balanced over me. Then we shifted positions and he had my leg up on his shoulder. We switched positions twice more before he had me on my knees, his hand gently pulling my hair as he thrust inside me from behind. My orgasm hit me just before he joined me in a chorus of moans. We both collapsed on the bed, completely spent.

I was out of it for a few moments until Wayne began to gently wipe me down with a warm rag. I turned over and smiled at him. "Thank you."

"I should be thanking you." He smiled. "But you're welcome."

I sat up while he went to put the rag back in the bathroom. My mind began to move rapidly. All I could think about was how I did not want a long-distance relationship. When he got back in the room I immediately got up off the bed. "I should get back to my room."

"You sure?"

"Yeah." I looked at his disappointed face. "This was amazing but I think we should just leave it at this."

"You're in a relationship?"

"No." I shook my head. "I just…"

"You don't have to explain." He smiled.

"Thanks." I started putting my clothes back on.

"Let me at least walk you back to your room."

"No. I'll be fine."

"Shayla, I just want to make sure you get to your room safely."

I sighed. "Okay."

We got dressed and Wayne walked me down to the elevator. We didn't say anything on the short ride to my floor. He walked me to my door and waved once I opened it. I watched him walking back to the elevator and silently cursed myself. He might have been worth it. I just wasn't willing to take the risk.

A month later…

I sat at the conference room table in a state of shock. The meeting was supposed to be an opportunity for us to meet the new management team that was taking over the firm. It turned out to be a meeting where we all got fired. The man was discussing severance packages but I was in such a daze I could hardly make out what he was saying. A woman passed out envelopes for all of us. I hoped it explained what he was talking about.

We knew that our firm was in trouble and would likely be taken over. All of us were prepared to have to get adjusted to new bosses. But as I looked around the room at my coworkers, I could tell that none of us expected to be fired. Had I known that I wouldn't have forced myself to get out of bed and go to work on a Monday morning. Who fires people on a Monday?

I glanced across the room and there was a guy who kept looking at me. He was standing behind the new team of executives, leaning on the wall like he would rather be someplace else. Under normal circumstances, I would have smiled at him because he was extremely attractive. Then I realized it was Wayne. The guy I met at the conference a few weeks earlier. My brain couldn't process that information so it pushed it right to the side. My mind did register how kissable his lips still looked for a brief second before I forced my attention back to the man telling us we needed to have our offices cleared out by the end of the day. Not that I had an office. Ten years with the firm and I was still in a cubicle doing twice as much work as the ones with office doors to close. I wanted to laugh as the meeting was adjourned and the grumbling began. Instead, I simply smirked as I walked out of the conference room and headed to pack up my belongings.

It wasn't as if I loved my job and was heartbroken about losing it. My primary concern at the moment I began to pull the pictures down off the side of my cubicle was my car note and mortgage payment. I was much more attached to my paycheck than I was to the firm. Granted, the paycheck wasn't what I wanted it to be. My attempts at advancement hit a ceiling when I got promoted to an HR associate from the clerk position I had held prior to completing my master's degree. The firm was great for encouraging me to take classes and go to training. They paid for the master's degree through their tuition reimbursement program. However, all that knowledge was sitting in my brain because they refused to promote me any higher. The best I got was to be able to fill in for one of the HR trainers when he was out on paternity leave.

"Excuse me."

I looked up from where I had been absentmindedly packing to see Wayne standing at the opening of my cubicle. "Yes?"

"I was coming around to collect resumes."

"Resumes?"

"Yes. In the meeting, we explained that we would have some openings and the displaced staff would have an opportunity to apply…"

"Oh. I'm good. Thanks."

"Excuse me?"

"I'm not interested in applying." I opened up the overhead cabinet and sighed. It was full of my books from school and training.

"Shayla, are you sure?"

I wasn't but something told me that I really didn't want to even attempt to keep working in the building. That was especially so if he worked there. I could smell just the hint of an earthy fragrance he was wearing and I had to fight the urge to stand closer to him. “Yes. I’m sure. Thank you though.”

He stood there for a moment longer and then walked away. A few minutes later someone appeared with boxes. Coworkers kept coming by to gripe but I didn’t let them distract me from getting my cubicle packed. I had it in my mind that I could break the whole thing down and be out of there before lunchtime. I glanced over at Dana to check on her. She was the one person in the building I actually talked to outside of work. She shook her head when she saw me. She was on her phone and tossing things into boxes. I knew we’d talk later.

I got all my things packed up by eleven. I was glad I never got as comfortable as some of my other coworkers who looked like they lived in their offices and cubicles. I was able to get all of my things in four boxes. The woman in the corner office was going to need a moving truck. I loaded my things onto the empty cart I found in the aisle.

After a quick stop to give Dana a hug and let her know I'd call her, I pushed the cart to the elevator.

"Shayla…"

I tried not to groan as I turned to face Wayne. "Yes."

"I just wanted to double check with you that you didn't want to leave your resume."

"I told you before I didn't."

He nodded. "Do you need some help?"

"Y'all in a hurry to get the place cleared?"

"No. I was just trying to be polite."

"You fire a bunch of people on a Monday morning and now you're trying to be polite." I rolled my eyes.

"I didn't fire…"

"Were you not in the room? I swear I saw you holding up the wall."

"Yes but…"

"Okay. So, you and your team fired a bunch of people." I cut my eyes at him and then pushed the cart on the elevator when the doors opened. He followed me on and I couldn't hold back my groan. "I promise I'm not going to steal your cart. You need me to bring it back up when I'm done with it?"

Wayne ran his hand down his face and then looked at me. "I can understand if you are upset…"

"I am beyond upset. I got up out of my comfortable ass bed to come in here and get fired. Now, instead of preparing for what was supposed to be a relaxing birthday weekend, I have to spend the week figuring out where I am going to be working so that my bills get paid."

Wayne sighed. "We are hiring some people…"

"I don't want to work for people who fire people on Monday. The shit is ridiculous." I knew I was being a bit extra but I was starting to really get upset.

“I happen to know a good headhunter. I could pass along your resume to her.”

“You are really pressed right now.”

The elevator stopped and the doors opened. Wayne sighed and handed me his card. “Here. If you change your mind about the job or me passing your resume along, give me a call or shoot me an email.”

I took his card and dropped it in my purse. “Can I go now?”

“Yes.”

I pushed the cart off the elevator and down towards the lobby doors.

“I can’t believe you didn’t have your resume already together.” Raven rolled her eyes and continued to do work on my laptop.

"I've been on my job for so long. How was I supposed to know I needed to have the damn thing ready?" I groaned and sipped my wine.

"If you stay ready you don't have to get ready." She shot me a side glance and then kept typing. "You needed to have been looking for something else years ago after the last promotion you got passed over for."

"Thanks for helping me feel better." I rolled my eyes.

"Listen, this was just the change you needed. Weren't you saying you wanted to switch it up now that you are about to be forty?"

"I meant I was thinking about cutting or dying my hair." I got up to pour myself another glass of wine.

"Well, clearly life was thinking about something else." Raven stopped typing. "Okay. So, this resume is gorgeous and we need to start sending it everywhere."

"Do we have to do it tonight?"

"You should at least send it to that guy you were talking about."

"What guy?"

"You said his name was Wayne."

"I'm not sending him my resume. He fired me."

"He didn't fire you. His company fired you. He offered to help you find another position and in this job market, you're going to need all the help you can get."

I groaned. "I don't want his help."

"Didn't you say he was cute?"

"Girl, he was the guy I met at the conference a few weeks back."

"Bitch what?"

"Yes."

"The one you refused to take any contact information from because you felt like it was a once-in-a-lifetime experience and it could only go downhill from there?"

"Yes. One and the same."

"This is crazy." Raven paused. "And he still looked good?"

"The most kissable lips ever." I almost gushed and then caught myself. "Do not try to distract me. I don't want to work for his company and I don't need him to give my resume to a headhunter. I can do that myself."

"Shay, stop being so stubborn. Every little bit helps." She reached out her hand. "Give me his card and I will craft a nice professional email to him stating that you're only forwarding him your resume so he can pass it along to his headhunter friends."

"Let me see this resume before you send it." I walked over to Raven and read over her shoulder. "You're really embellishing, aren't you."

"No. These are things you said you have done."

"But they weren't really part of my job."

"You did them at work so they were part of your job. You have done all the training to become a trainer so I don't see why you shouldn't apply for jobs that will allow you to use that knowledge." Raven gave me the side eye. "Don't sell yourself short. This is your chance to apply for all those dream jobs."

"I don't have enough savings to dream."

"Well, you will apply to other jobs as well."

"I don't know."

"Aren't you the one who encouraged me to apply for the management trainee program when I was stuck on just being an administrative assistant?"

"Yes but..."

"No buts. Don't make me call Alisha."

"I already sat on the phone for a thirty-minute pep talk with her."

"You might need another."

I sipped my wine. "Naw. I'm good for today."

"Where is she anyway?"

"I told her not to skip class for me."

"How many more of those does she have?" Raven sipped her wine.

"I think three. Then she will take her test to become a real estate agent."

"Don't think I forgot." Raven turned to me. "Where is that business card?"

I groaned and walked across the room to my bag. It took me a second to fish out the card from where it had fallen to the bottom. "I really don't think this is necessary."

"The man wants to help. Let him help."

"Whatever."

"Did he offer Dana the same help?"

"I don't know. She said she gave him her resume though."

"Call her."

"Chile, she is good and drunk by now. She texted me and said she was stopping at the liquor store on the way home."

Raven sighed. "I hope y'all get something soon."

"Me too. I got bills to pay."

"You good for this weekend?"

"Yeah. I paid what y'all gave me and my part for the cruise upfront."

"Hair and nails?"

"I'll need to get that touched up for interviews anyway so I'm not worried about that expense. Just can't go as wild as I want."

"Well, I think you still need to celebrate all weekend. We got you covered for brunch on Sunday."

"Awww, thank you, sweetie." I gave Raven a hug. "What would I do without you?"

"Chile, let me go so I can send this email. You ain't slick."

I laughed.

By Friday the reality of being unemployed had set in. I spent the week cleaning and purging my townhouse in between applying to all of my dream jobs. Tuesday and Wednesday I was very picky with what I was applying to. By Friday morning, I was telling myself that starting Monday I would be applying to every HR job that I could find. I had gone over my finances several times and knew that after a month I would be in trouble.

"Your father and I can loan you some..."

"No mommy." I looked at my parents. The years had them looking like two connecting puzzle pieces. Both had concerned looks on their faces while we ate dinner that Friday night. I sighed. "I'm not in need of a loan just yet. I just have to get on my grind and find a new job as soon as possible."

"I don't think you should have turned down the possibility of working for that new firm." My mother shook her head.

"Cheryl, her gut told her to pass on it." My father ate a bite of his steak.

"More like her pride." My mother sipped her wine. "She gets that from you."

I couldn't help but chuckle. "Mom, there wasn't going to be any growth for me there. They came in with their own team. At best I would have been shoved into doing the same thing I had been doing."

"What's wrong with that?"

"I wasn't happy." I looked down at my pasta before taking another bite.

My mother's eyes softened. "Well, I'm certain you will find an even better job soon."

"Your mother is right." My father smiled at us.

I shook my head at his attempt to get brownie points after disagreeing with her earlier. "I'm good on my bills for another month. If push comes to shove, I will have to just accept any job for a bit."

"You don't want to do that. If you need us to help, we will. I don't want you to get a job you hate." My mother frowned a little.

"Y'all are too close to retirement for me to be dipping into y'alls stash." I shook my head. Both of my parents were coming up on sixty-five and they had plans that I didn't want to mess with. They worked hard my whole life to build up the money to be comfortable and not have to work themselves into the grave. "I'll dip into my 401K before I get money from y'all."

"Babygirl…"

"Daddy, I will be fine." I sipped my wine. "Let's change the subject."

"How does it feel to be forty?"

I looked at my father and laughed. "A lot like thirty-nine, only a bit more stressful due to recent events."

He chuckled. "Forty is the new twenty."

"Daddy, forty is the new forty." I shook my head.

"What do you and the girls have planned?"

"Day party cruise tomorrow and brunch on Sunday."

"Sounds nice." She smiled. "I'm glad you didn't plan a big trip."

"Me too." I sighed. "Even though I could certainly use a getaway right about now."

"You'll have a great weekend celebrating. Try not to worry about things. Hit the ground running Monday morning."

I nodded and took another sip of my wine. I planned on taking my mother's advice because there was no way I wanted to be in the situation of having to borrow money from them.

"Excuse me but can I buy you a drink?"

I turned to the voice and smiled. He was a solid six. Maybe a seven if he had a better relationship with his barber. As single as I was, I had too much going on in my life to get caught up with someone who didn't make good life decisions. Picking a good barber is a life decision.

"No. But thank you for the offer."

"You sure?"

"We're drinking bottomless sangria at my table. I'm good." I smiled again and turned away. I thought I heard the guy start to say something else but Alisha came over and pulled me away from him.

"Chile. He was a four."

"I gave him a six."

"Four. Looking like he wiped his hands on his clothes when he came out of the bathroom." Alisha sucked her teeth. "Naw. We not doing that. Get back over here with us."

"Y'all the ones looking, not me." I said when I got back to our booth.

"Now you know I'm happy with hubby at home." Dana looked at me. "It's just fun to watch these negroes try to spit game."

Our friend Nicole came back from the dance floor and sat next to me. "He who must not be named is here."

I groaned. I knew she was talking about my ex. "You mean I'm trapped on a boat with him?"

"I will throw that bitch overboard." Raven looked around.

"You will not." I shot her a glance. "That's what he wants. Don't give him any attention."

"There were a lot of guys worthy of attention when I checked out upstairs." Alisha smiled.

I tried not to look around to see if I saw Keith. Instead, I refilled my glass of sangria and looked at my friends. Dana and I met at work when she got hired, six years earlier. We became friends after bumping into each other at the same happy hours. Alisha and I met in college. Nicole and I met through Keith. She was dating one of his friends when he and I started dating three years earlier. Neither relationship lasted but our friendship did. Raven and I had been friends since middle school. Her last name was Nance and mine was Moore so we ended up sitting next to each other in most of our classes.

I was thankful to have my girls celebrating with me. We celebrated everything together. We went to day parties, galas, football and basketball games, after parties, and brunches together. The great thing was that we never let our significant others get in the way of having a good time with our girls. That had been a big issue with Keith. He hated that I hung out and had a good time without him. When we invited him, he never wanted to come. After a year of that, I got tired and used the next available argument to break up with him. He had been trying to get back with me for the past two years.

"Oh, I see his egg head ass." Alisha casually tipped her glass in his direction.

I didn't immediately look but waited until the song changed up to glance. Then I groaned. I shook my head and decided to actually take a moment to look at the guys in the crowd. Alisha was right. There were a lot of solid sevens and eights walking around the room. "Y'all need to make some connections today. I'm tired of hearing y'all complain about being single."

Dana laughed. "Relationships aren't all they're cracked up to be."

"Bitch, you're happy. Stop playing." Nicole laughed. "Besides, Dre and I finally had the conversation so I won't be getting any numbers today."

"Wait. He was on his grown man and actually told you he wanted to be exclusive?" Raven asked.

"Yup. I was shocked. Whole conversation took me by surprise. One minute he is giving me the flats and taking my drums and the next minute he is telling me he doesn't want me to see anyone else."

"Awww."

"I've been married for five years and Eli won't give me his flats." Dana frowned.

"But you made sure it works both ways, right?" Of course, Raven was the one asking the important question.

"Of course. I told him that we needed to continue to meet each other halfway." Nicole smiled.

Her smile made me smile. I was happy to see my friends happy. I turned to Alisha and Raven. "So, ladies. Y'all gotta find the one."

"What about you?"

"I have too much on my plate." I sipped my sangria.

"Whitney's dad asked me out last night." Alisha said quickly before taking a gulp of her sangria.

"Whoa. Your baby father asked you out?"

"Whitney isn't a baby. She's eight." Alisha sighed. "Yes. He's back in town and said he wanted to take me out."

"Did you say yes?" I asked.

"I told him I would think about it."

"Bitch, tell that man yes." Raven rolled her eyes. "You know the only reason you weren't giving him the time of day is because he is in the service. Isn't he almost done?"

"He's transitioning out now."

I giggled when I saw the smile she was trying to hide. "Y'all make me sick. All this good news and y'all have let me be all depressed about work."

"I still don't know why you didn't apply for a position." Dana looked at me. "I mean I know why but it is better than nothing."

"Did they offer you something?"

Dana shook her head. "They said it would be another two weeks before they decided on anything. Eli told me to relax so I am just going to try not to stress and keep my eyes open for a position."

Raven glanced at me but she didn't say anything. I knew she was thinking about how Wayne said he would send my resume to a headhunter. She wouldn't say anything in front of Dana.

"Let's toast to not being unemployed for long." I raised my glass.

Dana raised hers. "I'll drink to that."

"Hey, Shay."

I glanced over my shoulder after we toasted and plastered on a fake smile. "Keith."

"Happy Birthday." He smiled at me.

"Thanks."

"Want to dance?"

"No." I turned back and looked at Raven. I needed to make sure she wasn't ready to toss him out the window of the boat. She was looking elsewhere and sipping her sangria.

"Um…"

Before Keith could finish, a guy I knew from parties came over and took my hand. I sat my glass down and proceeded to the dance floor with him. He was a great dancer, solid eight in looks, but married and he liked dancing with me because I never tried to push up on him. I was thankful for the save from Keith, who was still standing in the same place looking at me dance. I decided to ignore him and pray that Raven didn't snap. I couldn't remember exactly what he did to piss her off but she had been ready to pop him for quite a while.

"I'm trying to reach Ms. Shayla Moore."

"This is Shayla."

"Hi. This is Wayne Baker."

"Oh. Hi." I paused. I was already thrown off by how smooth his voice was. The fact that he was calling me pushed me further over. My mind immediately went back to the night we spent together.

"I was calling to see if you would reconsider coming back to work at the firm. We have a position similar to one that you held open."

"I'm still not interested."

He chuckled. "I kinda figured."

"Really?"

"I reviewed your resume. You're overqualified for the position. I just felt I still needed to offer it to you."

"Thank you for your consideration."

"I did keep my word. I passed your resume on to a friend of mine and hopefully, they will be in touch in the next few days."

"I appreciate that."

"How was your birthday weekend?"

"Excuse me?"

"When we talked you said you had birthday weekend plans. I remembered before you said you were hanging out with friends for your birthday. I hope you enjoyed yourself."

I was shocked at his memory. "Um… it was great. Thanks for asking."

"Well, with your marketable skills I'm sure you will get snatched up soon."

"From your lips to God's ears."

"Anyway, I won't keep you."

"Thanks again for passing the resume along."

"Not a problem. You're welcome. Have a good day and good luck."

"Thanks." I hung up the phone and stared at it. I could have listened to him talk for another hour or two. His voice was like a warm hug you want to sink into and stay forever.

Two days later, I got a call from the headhunter Wayne sent my resume to. We talked for about a half hour about what I really wanted to do with my career. Then she told me to pay close attention to my email and phone because she planned on sending my resume all over. The following Monday, I got called in for an interview. That job didn't pan out but it was the beginning of a steady stint of interviews. I had at least two interviews a week for three weeks. In the final week, I went on four interviews. By the end of it, I was frustrated and tired.

"Interviewing is a good thing. So many people's resumes just end up in the shredder." Raven tried to console me.

"I need one of these interviews to turn into a job. I have been out of work for a month. Bills are due and my savings is taking a beating." I groaned.

"Did you get the job leads I sent you?"

"You and everyone else I know. Hell, even Wayne sent me three last week."

"Wayne?" Raven paused. "As in old boy who you sent your resume to? The one who connected you with the headhunter? The one you said was amazing in bed but you weren't trying to stay in touch with cause you're a crackhead?"

"Yes." I rolled my eyes.

"I didn't know y'all were keeping in contact."

"We aren't really. I told you he called me about the job. That was it." I paused. "Well except for when he sends me job leads."

"That is sweet."

"Is it?"

Raven laughed. “Yes, it is. He doesn’t have to send you job leads. Clearly, he cares.”

“I guess.”

“Is he sending Dana job leads?”

“He doesn’t have to. She accepted the position.”

“Was it the one he offered you?”

“Yeah. Apparently, they only hired one person back from our section. She was it.”

“Shayla…”

“Don’t start.” I groaned.

“If you took that job, she wouldn’t have one.”

“I realize that.”

“Don’t tell her.”

“I wouldn’t dream of it. She felt horrible telling me that she was going back. She didn’t mind the work so much. She liked the routine of it.”

"You'll find something." Raven sighed. "You can't give up."

"I'm not." I paused as I looked at an email that popped up on my phone. "The headhunter got me another interview for Monday."

"Is the position interesting?"

I scanned the email. "Very. It looks like exactly what I want to do."

"Better make sure your power suit is clean."

"I need my roots tended to."

"I know the salon isn't in the budget right now. Why don't you come over Sunday afternoon and I can hook your head up?"

"You'd play with chemicals for me?" I laughed. Raven went natural back in college.

"If that is what you want to do then yes."

"I kinda want something more low maintenance."

"Oh, if you want to go that route, I can get my cousin to come over and she can cut it for you."

"I love you."

"I love you too Shay."

It was so cliche but cutting my hair off made me feel powerful. Raven flat ironed the hair that I kept in my new pixie cut style. The change gave me a much-needed boost of confidence when I went into my interview that Monday. I felt like I wowed them. I interviewed with a panel and we laughed for a large portion of the interview. The position was for a corporate trainer that would be responsible for not only new hire training but also in-service training for current staff. After the formal part, they walked me around to show me the office space and the classroom area. I felt great in my favorite black pants suit and new haircut. The interview ended as most had, with a handshake and them saying that they would be in touch. I didn't let it deflate me. I took my good mood and headed to meet Alisha for lunch.

"Look at you." Alisha grinned as she walked over to the table I was sitting in the cafe. "I am loving this look."

"Thank you. I like it too."

"You have the cheeks for this." She sat down. "How was the interview?"

"It went great." I sighed. "I'm remaining hopeful while still sitting here looking for new job listings on my phone.

"Tell me about this interview."

We ordered food and I gave Alisha the play-by-play of the interview. When I finished, I sighed. "This job sounds amazing so I'm hoping that something comes from this interview. I just don't want to get my hopes up."

"Understandable." She smiled at me. "Want to hear some good news?"

"You and Whitney's dad are getting back together?"

Alisha's eyes got wide. "Chile, what is wrong with you?"

I chuckled. "That wouldn't be good news?"

"I mean…" Alisha stammered.

"Well?"

"I don't know. We went on a date. I didn't tell Whitney about it because I don't want her to get her hopes up."

"Did you have fun?"

"Yes."

"Did you remember what you liked about him in the first place?"

"Yes." Alisha sighed. "That part is easy. The only thing that didn't work out was that I didn't want to be dragged all around the world."

"You like to travel."

"Travel, yes. Pack up and move every few years because of new assignments, no."

I sighed. "Well, I'm glad you had a good time. Are y'all going out again?"

"He wanted to do something as a family but I told him we weren't there yet. Now he is planning a second date."

"Good." I paused. "So, what was the good news? You passed your real estate test."

"Yes. That is my good news."

"That's awesome. Are you going to start working soon?"

"I got an offer to work with a firm but I'm still applying to join other firms. I think I need to start part-time."

"Yeah. You can't afford to just jump out there with a little mouth to feed."

"Timmy says that he can help out some more but I don't want him to do that."

I giggled. "That man is ready to wife you."

"Whatever."

"He is trying to retire from the military and wife your ass." I shook my head. "I love to see it."

Alisha tossed her napkin at me. "I can't stand you."

I got the call just as Raven and I were getting ready to head out for happy hour. She had just had the week from hell and left work early. I met her at her place and offered to be her designated driver. We were walking to her front door when my phone rang.

"Hello."

"Ms. Moore?"

"Yes."

"This is Ms. Lennox from Albright and Associates. We met on Monday."

"Yes. Hi Ms. Lennox."

"I know it is the end of the day but I couldn't wait until Monday. We would like to offer you the position of Training Facilitator to you. I can email you the information and you can let me know by Monday…"

"Oh, I accept."

"Great. I will shoot you the specifics via email and I'll give you a call Monday morning to go over things."

"That'll be great. Thanks."

"Enjoy your weekend."

"Thank you. You as well." I hung up the phone and looked wide-eyed at Raven. "I got the job."

Raven squealed. "That's awesome. I knew it."

I looked down at my phone when the email notification sounded. “She wasn’t playing. She just emailed me all the specifics.”

“This is great. We need to celebrate.” Raven paused. “Maybe I should drive.”

“Nope. I’m good. Two glass limit for me tonight. I’m going to want to go over this paperwork when I get home anyway.”

“Now all you need is a date and life will be wonderful.”

“I’m not worried about a date. I’m worried about how soon I’ll be getting this first paycheck.”

“Is it a raise?”

“It should be.”

“I’ll drive your car over and you can scan that paperwork. Are the rest of the girls coming?”

“Yes.”

“It’s a celebration bitches.” Raven took my keys from me. “Let’s go.”

My first day at work was a lot to process. The first shock was that not only did I have an office, but my office had a decent view of a park. Then the person training me was an absolutely delightful older woman. She had been a trainer for the company for fifteen years and was planning on retiring in less than a year. I was going to be shadowing her for several weeks before they planned on having me work on my own. It was comforting to know that I didn't have to reinvent the wheel. It was also great to see that they had a woman in the position prior. After being introduced around I noticed that the executive staff was fairly diverse and the atmosphere was just as comfortable as I thought it was during my interview. I kept my fingers crossed that it stayed that way.

I tried to field well wishes from my friends as they came in via text message. The headhunter even sent me a motivational email that morning. I was so grateful for the support system I had while I was looking for a job. Towards the afternoon I noticed that I had an email with a few job leads from Wayne. I realized that I hadn't told him that I had found a new job. I sent him a quick email telling him that I had secured a position and thanked him for all his help. A few minutes later my phone buzzed. I was in the middle of learning the company computer system so I didn't get a chance to check it for another hour. When I did, I had to smile.

Wayne Baker: Congratulations!

Shayla Moore: Thank you!

Wayne Baker: I hope you are going out to celebrate.

Shayla Moore: Not really. I celebrated when I got the call.

Wayne Baker: When do you start?

Shayla Moore: Today is my first day.

Wayne Baker: Perhaps you will let me take you to dinner to celebrate a successful first day.

I had to pause and stare at the message for a few moments. We were on a break while the IT person went to their office to grab a cord I needed to make my printer work. I wasn't sure what to make of Wayne's request but knew I shouldn't keep him waiting too long.

Shayla Moore: Dinner?

Wayne Baker: Yes. Do you like Hibachi?

Shayla Moore: Yes

Wayne Baker: Great. There is a place on the West side of town. Is that far from where you are?

Shayla Moore: No. It's perfect.

Wayne Baker: What time works for you?

Shayla Moore: Six

Wayne Baker: I'll send you the exact address and see you then.

I tried not to smile at the thought that I had a date for dinner. My plans had been to pick up take-out on the way home. Then I re-read the text messages. I could hear them in Wayne's voice. That put a big grin on my face. I fixed my face quickly when the IT person returned with the cord. No need for them to see me grinning like an idiot.

I arrived at the restaurant fifteen minutes early and sat in my car. At first, I was trying to make sure I looked presentable after a busy first day. Then I was trying to give myself a pep talk. At least five times I had to talk myself out of canceling the dinner date. I was nervous. I didn't know if this was just a friendly celebratory dinner or if it was an actual date. I wasn't sure what Wayne's intentions were. It was hard to gauge things. Wayne did not put up a fight when I told him that I wanted to leave our one night as it was during the conference.

We hadn't talked about where we were from and I think we both assumed that we were looking at a long-distance relationship. Then the circumstances of us meeting again just made things a bit confusing.

My heart sped up when I saw him getting out of a huge SUV. I knew that I hoped that this was a date even though I kept telling myself that I wasn't exactly interested in dating. My heart was interested in dating him. I took a few deep breaths and got out of my car.

Wayne turned and smiled at me when I walked into the lobby of the restaurant. "Hey."

"Hi." I smiled.

"Your hair looks great." He looked at more than my hair.

His gaze sent a warm feeling through my body. This was definitely a date. I smiled brighter. "Thanks. I needed a bit of a change."

The hostess led us back to a section. Even though there were a few other couples in the area we were seated with no one on either side of us. Wayne helped me out of my jacket and held the chair while I sat down. It was refreshing to experience old-fashioned manners.

He looked at me after the waiter took our drink orders. "So, how was the first day?"

I smiled. "It was busy but great. I'm excited about the team I work with."

"Are you doing the same thing you did previously?"

"No. I am actually going to be a full-time trainer."

"That's great."

"I'm excited. The trainer they have is retiring and I will be taking over for her in the next few months."

"You seem excited. I'm excited for you."

“I really am. I spent a long time not doing the things I had trained so hard to do. It was frustrating.”

“I’m even more thankful that you didn’t accept the position with us.”

“My friend Dana took the job. I’m glad she got it.”

“Oh, I have met Dana. She’s great.” Wayne paused. “Besides, if you took the job then asking you to dinner would have been frowned upon.”

I was glad the waiter came back with our drinks and took our orders. It gave me a moment to collect myself. Once that was done, I looked at Wayne. “So, what do you do for the firm?”

“Chief Financial Officer.”

“Oh wow.”

“It’s a family-owned business. My cousin is the CEO.”

“The one who fired us.”

Wayne looked down. “Yes. That’s him.”

“I thought about it and it makes sense. I can’t say that I’m happy about it but it did lead to me getting my ass in gear and getting a job that I really wanted.”

“So, you aren’t pissed at me.”

“No.” I smiled. “I’m not pissed at you.”

“Good.”

The chef arrived at the table and we sat back and enjoyed the Hibachi experience. I felt comfortable in the silence. Our conversation picked back up when the cooking was done. We talked about our favorite places to eat. Wayne was quite the foodie and it was nice that he had been to a lot of the places that I enjoyed. We didn’t have the exact same taste but we had a lot of favorites in common.

“This should make taking you out for dinner dates easy.”

I glanced at him but had a mouthful of food so I couldn't respond to what he said. While I chewed, I looked down at my plate. When I was finally able to speak, I looked up at him. "You want to have more dinner dates."

"Yes. I'm enjoying getting to know you. I knew you were beautiful the minute I saw you and your personality captivated me. I regret not asking more questions that night we spent together. I feel like I missed out on a month of getting to know you better. I'd like to continue to get to know you better." Wayne paused. "If that's okay with you."

I smiled. "I'd like that."

Wayne and I met up for two more dinner dates. Both dates were on a Monday night and both were directly after work. We would meet at the restaurant that we agreed upon, have dinner, hug goodnight, and then go our separate ways. I had found that some men were creatures of habit and was about to guess that this would be our pattern until he stepped outside of the box I was ready to put him in.

Wayne: Are you free tomorrow night?

Wayne: I know I just saw you but I'd like to see you again.

Shayla: I don't have plans.

Wayne: I'd like to take you to this new place that opened recently.

Shayla: Sounds good.

Wayne: Is it okay if I pick you up? Our reservations wouldn't be until seven-thirty.

Shayla: That's fine.

I sent him my address and then smiled. I was thankful for the shift in things. I didn't have a problem with the way things were, they just felt like they might not change. Him picking me up made it feel like a real date.

I got up and closed my office door. Then I sat back down and called Raven.

"You busy?"

"Girl no. I just finished going through my emails. What's up?"

I sighed. "So, he doesn't fit in the box."

"What box?" She paused. "Wait. He's switching things up?"

"He's picking me up tomorrow night for dinner."

"See. I told you he might have more up his sleeve."

"We shall see."

"Give that man a chance to show you what he's working with."

"Three dinner dates that were exactly the same except for the conversation and food."

"He is taking his time."

"We've already slept together."

"He is trying to do things in order now."

"I guess."

Raven laughed. "If you are just trying to get him in bed again you should just say that. I'm sure he will cooperate."

"That's not it."

"So don't rush things then."

"I'm too old to play the waiting game."

"Whatever heifer. This is why you never dated a lot."

"I want to know what I'm getting into."

"He told you. He is trying to get to know you." Raven sounded like she was chewing. "So how is the new job coming along?"

"Fine. What are you eating?"

"I had a damn lunchtime meeting so I'm now trying to eat this sandwich before my next meeting."

"Thankfully we haven't had any lunchtime meetings here."

"They're the worst." Raven sounded like she had taken another bite.

I laughed. "Go eat your food. I will call you later."

"We're still doing happy hour on Friday, right?"

"Yes ma'am."

"Okay cool. Talk to you later."

"Later."

Wayne and I had another lovely dinner with great conversation. We always had great conversations. It flowed all the way back to my place. For a few moments, we sat outside my townhouse and continued talking.

I paused the conversation by putting my hand over his. "Wayne."

"Yes?"

"Why don't you come inside."

"Okay." He smiled.

Wayne and I got out of his car and walked up to my front door. He stood behind me as I opened the door. When we got inside, we took our coats off and hung them on the hooks I had just inside the entryway.

"Do you want something to drink? Water? Wine? Vodka?"

Wayne laughed. "No. I'm good."

We sat down next to each other on my sofa. I had invited Wayne in because I wanted to talk to him. As I looked at him, the words escaped me and all I could do was lean forward and kiss him. He slipped his arm around my waist and pulled me close as his tongue slipped into my mouth. We hadn't kissed since that night at the hotel when we first met months ago. I was quickly reminded how good of a kisser he was. A few moments into the kiss, Wayne pulled me onto his lap. His hands gripped my thighs under my dress. I moaned into our kiss as his hands moved to my ass.

Wayne stopped kissing me. "Did you actually want to talk about something?"

My hands were already opening his pants. I grabbed his dick through his boxer briefs and gave it a squeeze. "I wanna talk about this."

His fingers slipped between my thighs and into my panties. "And this?"

I moaned and nodded as he slipped two fingers inside me. Then he began to massage my clit with his thumb. His free hand unzipped my dress while he planted kisses all over my neck. I pulled my dress over my head and tossed it to the side. Wayne immediately unhooked my bra and took one of my breasts in his mouth. As he played with my nipple, I felt my orgasm creep up on me.

"Wayne." I got out his name just before my breath caught and pleasure swept over me.

"That's it, baby. First orgasm of the evening." He went back to kissing all over my breasts. Once my breathing calmed down a little, he pulled down the throw blanket I had over the back of the couch. He turned me over and rested me on the blanket. After licking his fingers, he pulled my panties off and tossed them with my dress. "You taste so good."

Before I could respond, Wayne had his face between my legs. He pinned one leg against the back of the couch and tossed the other one over his shoulder. I had one hand on the back of his head and the other in my own hair as I enjoyed the ride his lips and tongue took me on. It wasn't long before I was moaning and crying out through another orgasm.

Wayne lifted his head and looked up at me when he finished. "Where is your room?"

I pointed to the hallway as I caught my breath. Wayne got up, helped me up, and then tossed me over his shoulder. I gasped. He carried me down the hallway to my room and gently sat me down on my bed. His strength shocked me and turned me on at the same time. As soon as he got his clothes off, I was off the bed and on my knees with his dick in my hands. I planted a few soft kisses on the tip before wrapping my lips around it. I kept things as wet as possible as I moved him in and out of my mouth. Wayne had his hand on just resting on the back of my head.

"Damn woman." He pulled me back.

I smiled at him. "I wasn't finished."

"You trying to have me have you up all hours of the night."

I stood up and Wayne kissed me. He slipped his arm around me and pulled me close to him.

"You ready for me?" He asked me after our lips parted.

"Yes." I went to my nightstand and pulled a condom out of the drawer. I sat on the bed, opened the condom, and put it on Wayne. Then I leaned back and spread my legs. He was on his knees on the bed and lifted me up as he eased inside of me. His thrusts were slow at first but the speed and intensity began to pick up. I arched my back even more as he gripped my hips and guided my motions. My orgasm hit me like a wave. Wayne's pace became erratic as he climaxed as well.

I turned on my side and looked at Wayne when he came back from the bathroom. "We need to do that more often."

He chuckled as he came over and gently wiped me down with a warm rag. "I'm sure that is something that we can make happen."

"I hope so."

"I want to spend much more time with you."

"I'd like that." I smiled.

After putting the rag back in the bathroom, Wayne helped me take the top blanket off my bed. We got in bed, under the sheet, and he held me in his arms. I rested my head against his chest and I remembered how short my hair was. That caused me to giggle.

"What's so funny?" Wayne asked.

"I cut my hair. Now you can't pull on it." I smiled, remembering our first night together.

"Oh, that's okay." He gently held his hand around my neck and kissed me on my cheek. "I can find other things to do with my hands."

I moaned and rocked my ass against him. "Can we stay up just a little bit later?"

His other hand slid between my legs. "I think we can do that."

In the morning, I sat on my bed and watched Wayne get dressed in his gym clothes. He had run out to his car to get his gym bag earlier before taking a shower.

"You're not one of those guys who lives in the gym, are you?"

He laughed. "No. I go maybe three times a week if I can remember."

"Okay."

"Listen." He sat down on the bed next to me. "I want to be clear with you about us."

I nodded.

"I want to see where things go with us. I want to take you out more often."

"And come over more often?"

He kissed me. "Much more often. I also want you to come over to my place."

"I'd like that."

"That night at the hotel I knew that I wanted to be with you."

"I didn't know we lived in the same town."

"We got lucky. I want to capitalize on that luck."

"So, when are we seeing each other again?"

"Whenever you want."

"I'm going to happy hour on Friday night."

"So am I."

"Afterwards?"

"Sounds like a plan to me." He kissed me again. "Let me get out of here. Don't go back to sleep or you'll be late."

I laughed. "I'm not. I'm going to get up and make breakfast."

"Next time I'll have a suit with me and can join you."

I put on my robe and walked Wayne to the door. He kissed me again before heading out the door. I smiled thinking about all the next times to come.

Raven passed around the shots. "Things are looking up for all of us so we gotta toast to that."

Alisha hurried over to our group and sat down. "Sorry, I'm late. Timmy dropped me off.

They are on their way to his mom's house. Whitney is staying over there for the weekend."

"He dropped you off but is he picking you up?" Dana handed her a shot glass.

"Maybe." Alisha rolled her eyes.

"Raven's got a third date with a cutie. Alisha and baby daddy are getting cozy. Dana's hubby got a promotion. Shayla and her man are getting serious. And Dre and I are moving in together. Cheers to that shit." Nicole raised her shot glass and then we all threw back our shots.

The lemon drop shot went down so smooth but had a bit of a kick to it. I sat my shot glass down and turned to Nicole. "Wait. So soon. Moving in?"

"My lease is up and he has all that space." Nicole sipped her water. "He's trying to move way faster than I am. This is what we agreed to."

"How fast is he trying to move then? A ring?" Dana asked.

"He has already started trying to discreetly ask me what I like. Like I don't know what he's thinking." Nicole shook her head. Then she looked at me. "You didn't have any trouble having the grown folks' conversation with your man?"

"We talked about seeing each other more often. Then he stayed over. The next morning, before he left, he was very clear about wanting a relationship with me." I smiled.

"So, you're coming to the company picnic then." Dana clapped her hands.

"He hasn't mentioned it yet but I might be." I paused. "How is work?"

"Great. The environment is a lot better than before. Some days it's even fun." Dana grabbed a fry from our communal basket of French fries.

"I think our forties are going to be better than our thirties." Raven flagged down the waitress. The waitress came over with a glass of water for

Alisha and then took her drink order. Then Raven continued. “We need to plan a trip.”

“I don’t have enough leave for a trip.” I frowned.

“Girl, by the time our schedules all sync up you’ll have some leave.” Raven turned to Alisha. “You gonna plan something with me?”

“Let’s see what we can put together.” She nodded.

“How’s the new job going?” Nicole asked me.

“It’s great. The woman I am replacing is already slipping into retirement mode. She has me leading a lot of the trainings and she just sits in. Then we meet afterward and she gives feedback. So far, she says I’m doing good. I think I can do better but she keeps saying I’m doing fine.” I grabbed one of the wings from the plate in the center of the table.

“We are always hardest on ourselves.” Dana looked at me.

“If she says you are doing good then you are doing good.” Alisha added.

The waitress came around with Alisha’s drink and Dana ordered another round of shots. Already on my second drink, I needed to check on my ride before I had a second shot. I could always order a ride but Wayne had said he would come and get me. When I pulled out my phone, there was already a text from him waiting.

Wayne: I’m not far from you so just let me know whenever you’re ready.

Wayne: No rush.

Shayla: Good cause we’re on our second shot…

Wayne: LOL. I gotchu.

Wayne: Enjoy yourself.

Shayla: Thanks

I put my phone back in my purse and noticed everyone was looking at me. “What?”

“Smiling while texting.” Raven raised her eyebrow.

“Musta been talking to her man.” Dana sipped her drink.

“Wayne’s picking me up later.” I looked at all the eyes still on me. “He’s out with his friends not too far from here.”

“I love seeing you happy.” Alisha smiled.

“Same” The rest of the ladies at the table began to nod in agreement.

The waitress came over with our shots.

"To many more happy moments for all of us." Dana held up her glass.

We all toasted glasses and then took our shot.

Thank you for reading.

Please leave a rating/review on Goodreads and Amazon.

Other works by Turtleberry

Standalone Books:

Are You Okay?

Nobody's Somebody

Happily Ever After

Lena's Chance At Love

Both Sides of Me

Days of Summer

The Friend

My Neighbor

On Break

Thirst Trap

Winters' Trio

Short Story Collections:

Sweet Turtleberry Jam Vol. 1

Sweet Turtleberry Jam Vol 2

Scott-Williams Family Series:

Catching Evie

Needs To Be Met

Whiskey Kisses

It For Me

One More Kiss

Finding Love

These Women Series:

Book One

Book Two

Book Three

Luminous Cruise Chronicles:

Love Unexpected

Boos & Booze Series:

Halloween Spice

Timber Mills Series:

Living The Dream

www.sweetturtleberry.com

https://twitter.com/turtleberry

https://www.facebook.com/SweetTurtleberry

www.ingramcontent.com/pod-product-compliance
Lightning Source LLC
LaVergne TN
LVHW050325160826
845677LV00014B/3541

9798848833232